Sports Build Character

CITIZENSHIP IN SPORTS

by Todd Kortemeier

FOCUS
READERS

FOCUS READERS

www.focusreaders.com

Focus Readers is distributed by North Star Editions:
sales@northstareditions.com | 888-417-0195

Produced for Focus Readers by Red Line Editorial.

Photographs ©: asiseeit/iStockphoto, cover, 1, 7, 26–27; andipantz/iStockphoto, 4–5; michaelbwatkins/iStockphoto, 8–9; Bill Haber/AP Images, 10; Ric Tapia/Icon Sportswire/AP Images, 12; John Locher/AP Images, 15; *Nothing But Nets*, 16; Chris Young/The Canadian Press/AP Images, 19; Jae C. Hong/AP Images, 20; FatCamera/iStockphoto, 22–23, 29; dolgachov/iStockphoto, 25

ISBN
978-1-63517-530-1 (hardcover)
978-1-63517-602-5 (paperback)
978-1-63517-746-6 (ebook pdf)
978-1-63517-674-2 (hosted ebook)

Library of Congress Control Number: 2017948103

Printed in the United States of America
Mankato, MN
November, 2017

About the Author

Todd Kortemeier is a writer and editor from Minneapolis. He has written more than 50 books for young people, primarily on sports topics.

TABLE OF CONTENTS

CHAPTER 1

What Is Citizenship? 5

CHAPTER 2

Citizenship in Action 9

CHAPTER 3

Citizenship and You 23

CHARACTER QUESTIONS

Are You a Good Citizen? 26

Focus on Citizenship • 28

Glossary • 30

To Learn More • 31

Index • 32

WHAT IS CITIZENSHIP?

US hockey coach Herb Brooks had a saying. The name on the front of the jersey is more important than the name on the back. A player's name goes on the back. The name of the team is on the front.

Most sports teams represent a city, state, or country.

Players and their team represent a **community**. They want to represent it well. But that means more than just playing well. It means being good **citizens**. Being a citizen is like being a teammate. A sports team works together to win. And citizens work together to help their community.

LET'S DISCUSS

What communities are you a citizen of? They could be large or small.

 Helping at a food bank is one example of good citizenship.

This could take the form of **donating** money. Or it could be donating time to work with a **charity**. Some players also work to raise awareness of important issues. There are many ways to be a good citizen.

CHAPTER 2

CITIZENSHIP IN ACTION

Hurricane Katrina struck in August 2005. The storm caused heavy damage to New Orleans, Louisiana. A few months later, Drew Brees joined the New Orleans Saints.

Hurricane Katrina destroyed approximately 300,000 homes.

 Drew Brees helps rebuild a home that was hit by Hurricane Katrina.

New Orleans was still trying to recover from the storm. Many buildings were ruined. Lots of people had lost their homes. Brees did his part to help the city.

He and his family bought a house in New Orleans. They spent time living in the community. They also donated time and money.

Brees raised money to fix a high school football stadium. He pitched in to **renovate** a youth center. His actions showed the city he cared.

LET'S DISCUSS

How do you think the people of New Orleans felt when Brees helped them?

 Mark Giordano works hard both on and off the ice.

Hockey player Mark Giordano plays for the Calgary Flames. He is the team's **captain** and plays defense. The Flames represent Calgary, Alberta. Giordano is a proud member of that community.

In 2011, Mark and his wife Lauren started a program with Habitat for Humanity. They helped build homes for **needy** families. But in 2014, they decided to launch their own charity. It is called Team Giordano. The charity works to help schools and students.

Team Giordano has donated more than $200,000 to help four schools.

Some of the money goes toward school supplies. Some helps pay for field trips. Giordano visits each school he helps. Sometimes he plays floor hockey with the students. And sometimes he takes kids to watch the Flames practice.

Giordano won the National Hockey League's Foundation

LET'S DISCUSS

Who benefits when an athlete does charity work?

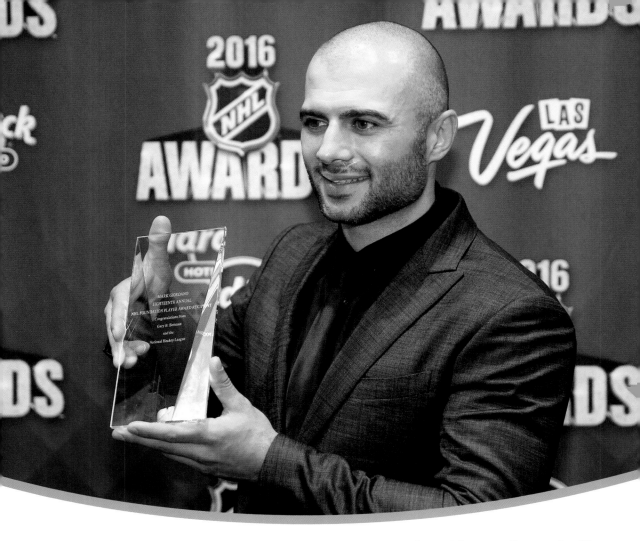

 Giordano holds the Foundation Player Award after the NHL award ceremony.

Player Award in 2016. It goes to

players who do important work in

their community.

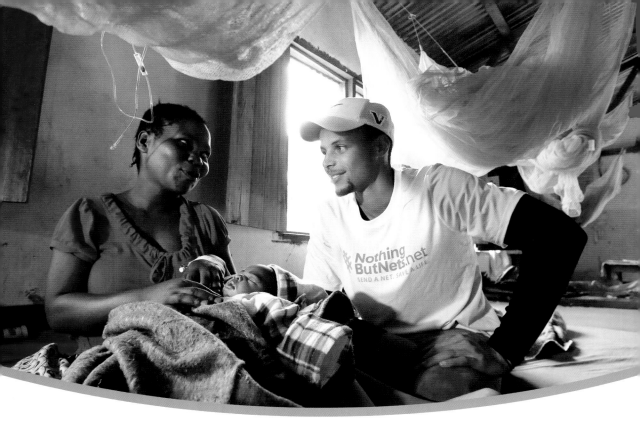

 Stephen Curry sits with a woman and child in Tanzania. Mosquito nets hang above them.

Basketball star Stephen Curry is known for hitting three-pointers. Each one means his team is three points closer to a win. It also makes three people in Africa very happy.

Curry takes part in the Nothing But Nets Program. Every time he makes a three-pointer, he donates three nets to protect people from mosquitoes. Mosquitoes in Africa can carry deadly diseases. By doing what he does best, Curry helps save lives. Curry has helped deliver the nets to Africa himself.

LET'S DISCUSS

What skills or interests do you have that you could use to help others?

Curry also helps organize a yearly event to help needy families. A group called Feed the Children donates food and personal items. Curry attends to hand out the supplies.

In 2017, Curry took time out of All-Star Weekend to help. The game was being held in New Orleans. Curry and other players helped build a school playground. Curry's actions show how he helps others, both at home and around the world.

 Stephen Curry shows citizenship by helping kids with their basketball skills.

 Williams (right) and her sister attended the opening of new courts in Compton in 2016.

Serena Williams made her first visit to Africa in 2006. The tennis star helped workers give medicine to people in need. Since then, Williams has been back several times. She has helped build schools.

Williams has also helped her hometown of Compton, California. Compton is a city that struggles with crime. Williams opened a building for families affected by violence. She also provided kids with school supplies. She believes education is an important part of citizenship.

LET'S DISCUSS

How can education help you become a good citizen?

CHAPTER 3

CITIZENSHIP AND YOU

Citizenship is a team sport. It takes everyone's effort. Athletes already know about teamwork. But some go the extra mile to become good citizens.

You can be a good citizen at school, at home, or wherever you go.

You don't need to shoot hoops to make a difference. You don't need to donate millions of dollars. Anyone can **volunteer** time to the community. And charities accept donations in any amount. They also collect food, clothing, and other items.

Playing sports is similar to being a good citizen. Everyone has a role. Nothing will happen unless everyone does his or her part. You don't need to be the star

 Caring for the environment is an example of good citizenship.

player. Even the stars need help sometimes. Every person has the ability to make the community a better place.

ARE YOU A GOOD CITIZEN?

Ask yourself these questions and decide.

- Do I do kind things for others?
- Do I have respect for the environment?
- Do I ever break the law?
- Do I work hard at school?
- Am I involved in community activities?

There are many ways to be a good citizen! Challenge yourself today to do one act of citizenship. You could pick up litter on your street. Or you could volunteer at the library.

Many people volunteer with family members or friends.

FOCUS ON
CITIZENSHIP

Write your answers on a separate piece of paper.

1. Write a sentence that summarizes Stephen Curry's charity work.

2. What kinds of charity work do you think are most helpful? Why?

3. How did Serena Williams help her hometown of Compton, California?

    A. She rebuilt homes after a storm.

    B. She donated nets to protect against mosquitoes.

    C. She provided kids with school supplies.

4. What do charities do with donated food and clothing?

    A. They give it to those in need.

    B. They sell it to raise money.

    C. They keep it for themselves.

5. What does **recover** mean in this book?

*New Orleans was still trying to **recover** from the storm. Many buildings were ruined.*

    A. to hide or take shelter
    B. to go back to normal
    C. to find a lost item

6. What does **organize** mean in this book?

*Curry also helps **organize** a yearly event to help needy families. A group called Feed the Children donates food and personal items.*

    A. to plan
    B. to attend
    C. to clean up

Answer key on page 32.

GLOSSARY

captain
A team's leader.

charity
An organization set up to help people in need.

citizens
People who live in a certain city or country.

community
A group of people who live in the same place or share the same interests.

donating
Giving a gift, often to people in need.

needy
Requiring help.

renovate
To restore something that is old or broken.

volunteer
To help out without being paid.

TO LEARN MORE

BOOKS

Herzog, Brad. *Awesome Stories of Generosity in Sports*. Minneapolis: Free Spirit Publishing, 2014.

Kopp, Megan. *Be the Change in Your Community*. New York: Crabtree Publishing Company, 2015.

Raatma, Lucia. *Citizenship*. Ann Arbor, MI: Cherry Lake Publishing, 2014.

NOTE TO EDUCATORS

Visit **www.focusreaders.com** to find lesson plans, activities, links, and other resources related to this title.

INDEX

A

Africa, 16–17, 20

B

Brees, Drew, 9–11
Brooks, Herb, 5

C

Calgary, Alberta, 13
Calgary Flames, 12–14
Compton, California, 21
Curry, Stephen, 16–18

F

Feed the Children, 18
Foundation Player Award,
    14–15

G

Giordano, Mark, 12–14

H

Habitat for Humanity, 13
Hurricane Katrina, 9–10

N

New Orleans, Louisiana,
    9–11, 18
New Orleans Saints, 9

W

Williams, Serena, 20–21